Stories

of

Life and Love

ELIZABETH CATHIE

LC

Lily Craske publishing

Printed in the United Kingdom
First printing, 2023
ISBN 978 1 916782 00 6

Cover image

To Mirriam

Enjoy

Elizabeth.

Dedicated to Sean

with love

LC

Lily Craske publishing

Contents

Susan's Echo

Tony sat beside the bed watching the midwife as she pottered around the room. He was forty-six years old - a bit thin on top, a bit wide round the middle - probably old enough to be her father, he thought to himself. Today, for the first time in his life, a child of his was about to enter the world. As he pondered this mysterious happening a memory – the shame of which had kept it buried deep in some hidden place for thirty years – bobbed, unbidden, into Tony's head. He was sixteen years old and it was the day of his Aunty Eva's wedding.

'Now our Tony,' said his mother as they waited in the drizzle outside the ugly concrete and steel of St Ambrose Church, the greyness of the weather matched by the greyness of the building, 'there'll be dancing at the reception. You're to dance with Cousin Susan. Not the whole time. I'm not saying that. But now and again,' Tony was silent, 'you hearing me Son?'

He'd kept quiet, imagining that silence would make the words go away; that silence would mean that he wasn't promising anything. Judith, Tony's mother, grabbed his arm and held it firmly, like the holding of the arm was the question. Their eyes met fleetingly, hers asking, unblinking, waiting for his response, his dodging around their sockets as he tried not to look at his mother, tried not to make real eye contact, desperate to look away but struggling to draw himself from the magnetism of her gaze. 'You hearing me, Son?'

Tony felt that this wasn't actually a question; that his mother was demanding the right response, the desired response. He felt that she was shouting, that everyone must hear, and he was embarrassed. But from outside the circle of his embarrassment he realized that no one else was listening, because no one else could hear.

'I'm hearing you mum, yes yes yes, I'm hearing you.' His mother called it his adolescent voice. She said it was sarcastic and whining. Sometimes he used it to annoy her, and sometimes he used it because it was just what came out of his mouth when he opened it.

'Aunty Judith, Aunty Judith come on into the photo,' the bride's voice broke the developing deadlock, 'come on our Tony, you're looking very smart, come on into the photo.'

~ ~ ~

'Rub my back for me would you Tony; there's a love.'

Tony rubbed Gill's back. How could one small baby take so long to arrive? Funny, he'd never really given it much thought until they'd landed in the delivery room in the middle of the night. Other people had babies and they just seemed to appear. You got a phone call or a message or one of those cute little cards with a cartoon baby on the front. You went round to visit with a bottle of something celebratory and a gift. You admired the sleeping bundle and congratulated the parents. Then you got out quick once the bundle began to squawk, or when unpleasant nappy aromas started to drift around.

Tony stumbled over his own feet when he made way for the midwife. He thought of her as someone in authority and people in authority made him feel awkward and bumbling. He made a trip to the coffee machine and sat down in an uncomfortable chair in the corridor. He'd drunk so much coffee in the past twelve hours that his brain was zipping around the walls and ceiling, leaving his body dozing and dreaming in the chair every time he sat down.

~ ~ ~

The reception was in full-swing. Speeches had been made and toasts had been drunk. The buffet had been eaten. Tony knew, without previous experience to inform him, that he was now officially drunk. It felt lovely, gentle and floating; it felt smiley and warm. He heard himself talking eloquently and intelligently to proper grown-ups. Some people laughed, he laughed with them. One man said, 'if you say so, laddie, if you say so,' and he'd replied, 'I do say so. I do say so.' Someone else said, 'well now, I do declare young Tony's drunk,' and it had seemed amusing to reply, 'well now, I do declare my good man ….. I believe that I may be ….. just a little bit …… tiddly. Well spotted, my friend …… well spotted.'

The man began to talk to someone else and Tony turned around - slowly in order to let his brain keep pace with his head, or maybe it was his head and his body that were out of sync, he wasn't quite sure which. As he turned there was his mother right in front of him. He waited for his eyes to readjust, so that he was just looking at one of her and began,

'Well hello there hello .....' but she grabbed his arm, put her mouth by his right ear and said - rather too loudly for Tony's current head situation - 'Time to dance with Susan, our Tony.' A feeble protest struggled slowly from his brain to his mouth. 'Oh but Mum, no....'

'Now Tony.' Tony registered that she was doing that thing again; shouting at him in a way nobody else seemed to hear. 'Now Tony.'

'Well Mum, you know, I don't think I will.' Suddenly, and without warning, Tony felt anger leap into his head, uncontrolled and unbidden.

'No I won't.' His voice was alarmingly loud, somehow out of his control. He tried to shove it back inside his head but it was loose now - loose and dangerous.

'Yes you will Tony.'

Now Tony was shouting, really shouting, not like his mother's pretend shouting. 'No mother. I won't. NO. I. WON'T.'

He hit out at the arm that was holding his. Then he hit it again and again and again. His mother let go of him. He saw her face, startled, alarmed, maybe even scared. They weren't a hitting family. Tony's world was spinning round, like when he got off the fast rides at Alton Towers and couldn't walk straight, and everyone laughed. The remembered laughter muddled itself with his unfamiliar head noises, and through it all he registered that the two of them – gangly teenager and middle-aged woman - were now surrounded by a circle of silence; a fence of curious onlookers. When he next opened his mouth the loudness of his voice and the ugliness of the words in the growing, deepening, silence were catastrophic.

'No Mum no. I won't dance with her. She's a freak, a Mongol. I won't dance with her. I won't.'

His mother turned and walked away.

~ ~ ~

'Time to come back in. Won't be long now. Baby's almost here. We're doing splendidly.'

The midwife managed to make the word baby sound like the approaching child's name. Gill was bathed in sweat, pale against the whiteness of the hospital bed. She clung onto his arm through the contractions, approaching the whole event stoically as he'd known she would. His sensible, practical Gill who'd had her hospital bag packed for weeks with exactly what was on the list. Who'd painted the spare room lemon-yellow and peppermint-green, installed a cot, and created a neat pile of unisex baby clothes out of what seemed to be a piece of fabric, a ball of wool and some ribbon. 'Our baby will have special things, specially made by me,' she'd declared, patting her tummy, 'no posh stuff and no supermarket finest for our new arrival.'

'Push.... Push.... Push.... That's it; you're doing well, really, really well. Wonderful. Keep pushing – brilliant.'

The midwife exuded an aura of calmness around the room. She was young and what his mother would call sturdy, thick dark hair platted through with red ribbons hanging down her back, large lime-green glasses looking jokey and out of place in the harsh lighting and amidst the medical bits and pieces. She smiled rarely, but Tony had come to realise over the past hours that, when she did smile, her smile connected with Gill in a way that inspired confidence, in a way that said, 'we can do this together, you and me.' The smile made Tony feel excluded.

'OK, is there another contraction? Right push push - keep pushing keep pushing, that's great, you're doing brilliantly. Ok, here's baby's head. I need you to stop pushing now, breath quickly, little breaths …… that's great …… wonderful ……brilliant. Now, are you ready?' there was the secret smile again, 'baby's nearly here, one last push …… that's it, well done, here we are …..'

'It's a little girl, well done, you did splendidly. It's a little girl, Dad - congratulations.'

Tony felt euphoric. There it was; lying on top of Gill. There she was, his little girl, his baby daughter, tiny arms and legs, miniature hands and feet, wrinkly red face squashed into Gill's body, little skinny bottom stuck in the air. He was scared to touch her, he felt so big and clumsy and she looked so small and breakable. Gill had turned into a mother cat, stroking the tiny body, talking to her, purring to her, saying hello, it's so lovely to meet you, I'm your mummy.

~ ~ ~

Gill was dozing, fresh and showered in practical Gill like fashion. Tony felt crumply; a bit sniffy. He thought he was probably wearing socks he'd taken out of the laundry basket. The baby – somehow that had become a name, temporary but a name all the same – lay snuffling and sleeping encompassed by Gill's arms; their heads close together sharing tiny kisses and secrets. The baby had been inspected by the midwife and by the doctor, and now the little family – 'my little family,' Tony mused - were in a side room on the maternity ward.

Tony thought he had never felt so tired. Reality and dream world began to mingle into each other in his head, and he could no longer stop his eyelids from closing, then opening, then closing again, in some kind of primeval, pre-sleep ritual. It was a journey into dream-world which couldn't be resisted.

'I'm your mummy, sweetheart,' he heard Gill say. Except that the voice wasn't Gill's soft, gentle, new-mother tones but his own mother's angry voice. And then the voice wasn't directed at the new baby, but at a baby Tony. But baby Tony could hear and understand. Then baby Tony morphed into a huge, gangly teenager, a monster, a giant, and now teenager Tony was shouting and shouting and there was Susan in a green and yellow party dress holding a baby close to her, rocking the blanket wrapped bundle, and he knew it was his new baby, and the dream-world Susan was calling, 'Tony Tony look Tony, baby. Love you Tony, love you,' except that the words never came out loud and she was crying and crying and the tears soaked the dress and somehow Susan deflated and crumbled and was no longer there, and teenage Tony was shouting, 'no no the baby where's the baby,' while grown up Tony was trying to call to Susan, who now seemed to be called Sylvia, but the words wouldn't come out. He was trying to move, trying to reach her but his dream legs wouldn't work; they ran and ran but didn't move. Now in place of Susan/Sylvia there was his mother and he wanted to call her but he couldn't. Then she turned and walked away.

'Tony Tony, are you awake love?'

Gill sounded bright, happy, 'the doctor's here Tony, wake up love.' She rearranged the baby in her arms and propped herself up against the pillows. The midwife came into the room and the two of them –fledgling new mother and hardy professional - held hands and said well-done and thank you and you did brilliantly and so did you. Then they laughed together and smiled their secret smile again.

'Have you decided on a name for baby?' the doctor asked without preamble, looking from Gill to Tony.

'Annie,' said Gill, 'we're going to call her Annie.'

'Annie', the doctor smiled, 'well now, isn't that a grand name; after the blessed Saint Anne maybe?'

Anger stirred in Tony. He wanted to ask why the doctor thought he could make their choice of name religious when it wasn't. But there was practical Gill holding his eyes with her own and saying,

'After my grandmother. She died last Christmas. We're calling Annie after her.'

'Well now, your Annie is fit and well,' the lack of preamble jarred inside Tony's exhausted head, 'you can take her home tomorrow. But everything is not quite as it might be. Annie is a special baby. You see here on her hand? She's missing a crease in her palm.'

Tony looked at the baby's hands. They were so tiny he didn't really understand what the doctor meant but he was too stubborn to say so. He just nodded and looked at Gill who was looking trustingly at the midwife.

'And see here around her eyes? There's not so much skin and crinkles as other babies have.'

Tony looked into the baby's little open, trusting eyes. And he saw Susan. Suddenly the floor was coming up to meet his whirling head. His stomach was coming up to meet his mouth. Words screamed around inside his head,

'A Mongol! Oh my God she's a Mongol.'

But that the words couldn't be contained in his head. They burst out and ricocheted around the walls and the floor and the ceiling on a journey of pain, until they slammed into the ears of Gill and the doctor and the midwife, bouncing, bouncing, until they burst into the tiny new ears of Annie - and ended their journey.

After the silence, the midwife fixed her gaze on him. 'Tony, that's not a word we use nowadays. Your baby, your Annie, has Downs Syndrome. She is fit and healthy, but she has Downs Syndrome.' She didn't share her secret smile with him.

Tony felt Gill holding his arm, anchoring him to the chair, her eyes pleading with him to stop, to listen, to think, to love, but he broke free with a violent twist of his body. And then he was gone from the room, leaving Gill to trace her fingers around Annie's eyes, to hold her tiny hand and kiss it, to purr into her neck, 'Mummy loves you' and 'you are so very precious' and 'Daddy will love you too. I'll show him how. I promise, little one, little Annie, I promise I'll show him how. Trust me sweetheart, trust mummy.'

~ ~ ~

At home Tony sits on the rocking chair in the

little candy stripped nursery. His body feels wrung out. His head feels like there will never again be a time when it doesn't hurt. His heart is broken - for Annie, for Gill, for Susan, for himself. He holds a fluffy smiling teddy in his hands and looks at the cot, waiting ready by the window in anticipation of Annie's arrival. Once again words come jumping from his mouth unbidden; angry words, sorrowful words, words wrenched from his overburdened heart.

'Who will dance with Annie?'

'Who will dance with Annie?'

Then we can all truly dance

Love her - she is our Annie,
a part of you, a part of me.
She'll make us laugh, quietly perhaps,
maybe uproariously, who can know.

She'll make us cry - for sure,
when she's hurting, when she's sad,
with frustration at her difficulties,
with pride at her achievements.

Our hearts ache now,
but she will be our blessing,
her arms will reach for us,
her heart will love us.

Look into her face - see Annie,
all that she is and will become.
Know yourself blessed.
Then we can all truly dance.

Mother and Daughter

10th January 2012

'You're not Bridget Jones,' my mother yells at me across the kitchen, 'why can't you get yourself married?'

'I know I'm not Bridget Jones,' I yell back just as ferociously, 'I don't want to be Bridget Jones and anyway Bridget Jones is out of date now, old-hat, gone, forgotten.'

'Like you,' came the bitter retort as my mother banged the pastry she was making down on the work surface, sending a cloud of fine flour dust over her face and hair, 'like you forgotten, on the shelf, an old maid.'

'Oh Mother!' Now I'm exasperated with her, 'nobody says those things anymore. There's nothing wrong with not being married; it's the new normal!'

'But I want you to be married,' she pleads, putting down the vegetable knife that she'd just been waving in the air in-between slicing up apples for the pie, and wiping her hands on the tea towel. 'I want you to be married, I want you to be happy; you're thirty-seven' - my mother's probably the only person who can make thirty-seven sound like pension age - 'and not even the shadow of a boyfriend for years now. You've given up, you've got too comfy with your nice job and your little house; spending all your time gardening and keeping those smelly cats company. I swear it's since you became a vegetarian. It's not good for you. I've always said so. Men don't like it you know. They want to know you're going to cook them a nice bit of meat for their dinner, not rice and lentils and chick peas. They want proper food.'

Where does she get these ideas? It's like she's stuck in the 1960's. All the men I know are perfectly capable of cooking for themselves and half of them are vegetarian. And come to think of it, most of them like cats which, I want to tell her, don't smell; it's dogs that smell. But I don't say these things. The day is too precious for another round of the same, 'why is there no boyfriend in sight,' argument with my mother. Instead I move closer and sit opposite her on the high, white, wooden stool that I always loved to sit on when I was a child helping her with her baking. I take up the piece of pastry which has, I observe, suffered badly from being on the end of her frustration, and place it carefully over the apples in the dish, pressing down the edges with my thumb to make a pattern like she taught me. She watches me, and I say a bit feebly and, I suppose, a bit predictably, buying time or release from conflict maybe.

'I just haven't found the right guy yet mum. I need to be sure. I can't just marry anyone can I? It's important. It's forever. It's got to be The One.' Even as I'm speaking I'm hearing the words hurtling out of my mouth and filling the air between us. Then almost to myself I ask, 'it has hasn't it? It's got to be The One. Can't just be anyone can it?'

She's upset. I know she's upset because now she's sniffling quietly into the sleeve of her jumper, and bustling around the kitchen taking things out of cupboards and wiping them with the damp cloth she's taken from the sink, then putting them back in their strictly assigned places again. She's always upset when we have these conversations, and we have them often - the kitchen cupboards are very clean. But I like my life the way it is. I can't get married just to please my mother; that would be weird.

'Rachel,' calm now, calm and sounding almost reasonable; 'you work in that huge hospital every day of the week. There must be eligible men round every corner. Just keep looking. Promise me you'll just keep looking, please?' She looks at me pleadingly - defeated, dejected, and so, because I love her, I do promise.

'I'll keep looking mum, I promise, I'll keep looking.' Then I say quietly, 'round every corner,' and she laughs a tiny wry laugh and learns her forehead against mine across the worktop. We stay like that for a moment looking into each other's eyes, both brown and both shiny with tears. We are so alike in so many ways, and so different in so many others.

Having promised, and so reached something of an uneasy truce for today at least, I feel that I'm allowed to leave. I hug her close. She smells of familiar perfume and cooking and the coffee we've just drunk. I kiss her cheek. She holds my face between her hands and kisses my nose, just like she used to when I was a child. I take the tea towel and wipe away the dusting of flour from her face, then brush my hands over her hair so the flakes of flour fall to the floor.

'See you at the weekend. Tell dad I'm sorry I missed him.'

'Bye-bye Rachel darling. Remember! You can always bring your friends here. It's still your home. I like to meet them.'

I don't reply because I know that what she really means in those stilted phrases is, 'please please please bring a nice young man here for me to inspect very soon'. I swear she won't give up her endeavour until I am drawing my pension, and probably not even then. I trudge home through the strange comfort of the dark, cold, frosty streets to my own warm, cosy little house with its neat garden, the vegetable beds at the front waiting patiently for spring, and my beautiful ginger cats sleeping curled together on the sofa, put on my pyjamas, and make a nice lentil and tomato pasta bake for dinner. It is my full intention to spend all of my winter evenings just like this; pyjamas, books, nice food, glass of wine, sleeping cats for company. There will be no pubs or clubs or internet dating or husband-hunting for me.

~ ~ ~

10th August 2013

Here I am in my wedding dress stood at the door of the old weather-beaten church. Actually I'm stood just inside the stone porch out of the rain, which is tumbling from an angry purple sky after a summer filled with glorious sunshine and long hot days. The rain doesn't matter to me and - thanks to some very large umbrellas and some surprisingly nifty footwork from car door to church door - I'm only a teeny bit damp round the edges.

No, the rain can't spoil this day. I'm just happy to be here; to have finally met The One. I'm happy to be having my once in a lifetime big day. I'm just truly happier than happy. There's a little group of musicians at the front of the church playing cheerful songs on violins and clarinets. I can just hear the murmur of muted conversations through the closed inner door, and I can sense that the atmosphere in the church is light-hearted and carefree.

It's not quite like that in the porch. My mother, who is stood beside me, believes I feel sure, that the ferocious rain is some sort of an omen. A bad omen obviously; probably sent by God. Not that she normally has much truck with the Almighty, but he's definitely getting the blame for this one. Because my mother believes I am about to make a big mistake. To my mother Sam, my lovely Sam, is definitely, irretrievably not The One. Which must be why, I suddenly realize, she's wearing the same hat that she wore to my brother's wedding. It's dark blue with little pink silk flowers on the brim and, now I look closely, I see that it doesn't quite tone with her light blue suit. In fact, now I look really closely, I'm not entirely certain that the suit is new either.

'Please, mum, go and sit down now,' I'm trying to stay calm but the porch is getting oddly claustrophobic, 'the Vicar wants to start the service. It's not right to keep everyone waiting like this. They'll start to think something's wrong. They'll think I'm not here, or they'll think Sam's not here.'

Some late guests squeeze past our tense little huddle, holding sopping umbrellas at arm's length, full of apologies and scuttling inside to find seats. I need my mother out of the porch. I need her out of harm's way. Sam and I are going to walk into church together and Sam is stood beside me listening, but pretending not to, to everything my mother says. And she's saying way too much for my liking.

At last she admits defeat, summons up all her dignity, and it is considerable, plasters a big smile across her now blotchy face, takes my brother's waiting arm, willfully ignoring the pained and impatient look on his face - shaved smooth for the occasion - and lets her handsome son escort her to her seat on the front row. I notice from my back of the church vantage point that he sits on the outside seat by the aisle; successfully corralling my errant mother between himself and my father.

I hear the vicar's clear confident voice over the PA system welcoming everyone to St Anne's on this beautiful summer's day. Everyone laughs, and the laughter is mingled with a sudden searing flash of lightening and a huge clap of thunder. There are more umbrellas in church than there are hats, and several expensive hairdos are clearly not going to recover in time for the photographs.

Then the organist starts to play and everyone stands up, and the bold ones, or maybe they're just the impatient ones, turn round to the back to watch us walking in. We've chosen the Allegro from Handel's fourth organ concerto to walk down the aisle to. Sam chose it. I don't know anything about this kind of music, but Sam plays the cello in an orchestra. Funny that! In the end I didn't meet him at the huge hospital, but at a tiny charity concert in the community hall that I'd only gone to to keep my best friend company.

Sam takes my hand, long, thin fingers gently but confidently holding my short, chubby fingers, thumb caressing my thumb in our familiar way. I look up and we smile at each other and then almost without realizing it we're walking side by side down the faded blue carpet of the aisle; past pink and white flower displays and big ivory candles with golden bows on, and past the people; lots of people. I don't really notice who's there; it's just a sea of faces smiling at us.

Everything's a bit of a blur but we must have passed my mother, in fact we must have passed everyone standing in their places to greet us, all our family and friends who've come to share this day with us, because here we are at the front of the church and Reverend Lucy is beaming down at us from her vantage point two steps up, reassuring us with her calm voice that this will all go beautifully.

And it does. I hear my mother crying gently behind me. But that's ok! Crying at their daughter's wedding! Isn't that what mothers are supposed to do? Isn't that what all mothers do? The service flows along. There are hymns, readings, prayers and it's all lovely; deeply personal, meaningful, and amazingly lovely. I feel that I'm enjoying this whole thing, and I feel that Sam's enjoying it just as much; stood tall and straight beside me exuding confidence which I can feel spreading over me as well. It begins to feel like magic, like a beautiful spell being wound around just us two, binding us together forever.

'Now,' says Reverend Lucy quietly just to me and Sam, 'we've come to the part where you make your vows to each other, so turn and face each other - that's right - people want to see what's happening. Now Rachel, you take Sam's hand and then just repeat the words after me.

But say them to Sam, not to me. It's Sam you're marrying, not me!' Sam and I both smile at this oddly reassuring little remark, because Lucy said the same thing when we came for the rehearsal last week. 'Remember you're marrying each other you're not marrying me. Talk to each other not to me.' I thought I'd forgotten everything about the rehearsal but I remember that, and I remember how lovely she was to us both.

'So Rachel,' Reverend Lucy says, and now I'm holding Sam's hand tightly and concentrating hard, 'you go first and just say the words after me.' I take a deep breath and look up into Sam's rich dark eyes which are looking expectantly down at me.

'I Rachel Louise'

'I Rachel Louise'

'Take you Samuel Paul

'Take you Samuel Paul

'To be my husband'

'To be my husband'

And the mother said

And the mother said to her daughter,
with a bitterness futile and helpless,
he is not the one
I would have chosen for you.

And the daughter, holding her mother
in a tender embrace, replied,
he is the one of my choosing;
we are grafted in love and hope.

Across the Generations

August 1994

The two figures walk along the road holding hands. The mother is short, not slim, wearing safe comfortable clothes and flat shoes, eschewing any notion of fashion, happy in her own body, confidence displayed unknowingly in her quiet voice and easy walk. She looks calm, almost serene, except that she is too ordinary to be serene.

The boy is small, just four years old. He walks happily by his mother's side doing little skips and hops, chatting just because he can. He has a blue, woolly hat pulled down over his ears. The summer day doesn't really merit the hat, but to those passing on the street or standing at the windows, who know the ways of children and can happily accommodate their oddities, the hat wearing can be seen for what it is, a loved garment whose wearing gives the child pleasure, something that by the time winter comes around again will have been discarded in favour of a new novelty.

The pair appears to dance along the pavement, happy in each other's company. When the child stops to push his face deep into a rosemary bush in a front garden, causing a buzzing and fluttering of disgruntled bumble bees, the mother laughs and waits as the space around her fills with the scent of the herb, until the boy is done with his game. Then briefly they hold hands again. Soon his happy voice echoes around the walls of the cul-de-sac as the door of the last little cottage opens. A man appears on the doorstep, drawn out by the sound of the boy's voice. Now the little boy's legs, in their red shorts, are running along the pavement, and his arms are spinning and weaving the air in joy.

'Granddad, Granddad, I'm here Granddad.'

The boy jumps and the man catches him. The boy wraps his skinny arms around the man's neck and his legs around the man's body and squeezes as tightly as he can, teeth clenched with effort. The small, smooth cheek presses against the rough, aging one, and they hold each other close. The boy wriggles around to hold the man's face between his hands and plants a kiss on his mouth.

'I'm here Granddad. Did you miss me?'

The man lifts him down to the ground, hunkers down beside him, holds his arms gently and, laughing, he plants his own kiss on the top of the boy's head.

'I missed you, Lad. I missed you.'

As their heads rest gently together in an act of love that transcends generations, the man thinks, 'you two are all the world to me, you and your mum.'

But the boy is four and stillness doesn't come easily to him, and now he's off inside the house calling for the dog,

'Sandy, come and play. Where are you? Come and play.' Frenzied barking from the garden sends the boy out through the kitchen to the back door, in search of his playmate.

The man straightens up.

'Debbie, hello: how are you?' his voice is gentle, caring, enquiring.

Debbie is not his daughter. She came into his life almost by accident, but he has come to love her dearly, and it is because of her that he has this boy - his grandson - to cherish. Debbie smiles at the man, feels the dryness of his skin and his lips as he takes hold of her hand, rests it against his cheek, and then kisses it.

'I'm well Tom thank you: very well.'

'And the boy - how's the boy?'

She laughs, puts her hands on his shoulders and looks into his eyes,

'He's happier for seeing you Tom - always happier for seeing you.' She treasures beyond all else this bond that her son has with his grandfather; the bond of a fatherless boy and a childless father.

~ ~ ~

Four years earlier

Tom is standing in the spring sunshine uncomfortable in his too warm funeral clothes, staring uncomprehendingly into the hole in the ground that now bears the long wooden box that holds – from this day forward and for all eternity – the forty-two year old body of his beloved son; his only child. Beneath this coffin is another, the one that holds the now decaying body of the son's mother. It is no consolation to Tom that in the shared experience of death they now lie reunited.

People pass by and words are offered, 'so sorry Tom,' 'so sad,' 'so young.' The black clad figures are shadowy, indistinguishable from each other - many young like Peter, unknown to Tom, all quiet, all respectful, most sorrowful, none cheerful. There are handshakes, brief squeezes of his shoulder, hands laid gently on his back in passing care and caress; colleagues, friends, neighbours; no family. They were their own tiny family of three and now there is just him, how can he be a family of one?

'Mr. Johnston. Mr. Johnston. Tom.'

The voice is confident, quiet and oddly female after the procession of young men. Tom sees a short woman, younger than Peter, pale face surrounded by dark curls tossed about by the wind. She looks into his eyes. She steps closer to him. She holds out a hand and somehow his hand is encased within it, not in formal greeting, not in formal grief, but a hand offered in comfort and consolation; a human touch offered and accepted. She is not afraid of his grief. She is strong enough to meet it face to face and not back away. Others have left the graveside and stand in groups chatting and smoking. Relief is palpable, 'the service is over and the old man hasn't fallen apart,' hangs unsaid in the air. Occasional laughter travels on the wind through this land of the dead in which they all trespass.

'I'm Debbie,' the eyes search his face for recognition of the name, 'I was Peter's new girlfriend.'

'Debbie, yes, Peter talked about you. Said he was bringing you to meet me. Sent me a photo of you. Sorry, I didn't notice that you were here.' Old fashioned politeness struggles through the veil of grief, and the oddity of his words strikes him. Why would she not be here, all Peter's other friends are here? She laughs briefly.

'I didn't expect you to,' but the laugh is not offensive or wrong. It's a laugh of reassurance and it does what it's intended to do. It connects them, Debbie with Tom and Tom with Debbie, and then their arms are around each other. He feels her round body with its strength and confidence. She feels the unfathomable depth of sorrow encased in a frailty he hadn't known was there, but that he now feels unleashing itself. He feels the curly hair against his neck, the strong young arms gripping him. She feels the masculine clothes against her face, and the man's hand holding her head. Comfort and grief mingle in the embrace of strangers.

She holds his hand as they walk past the other graves back to where the big black funeral car waits for its single passenger. Most people have gone now, on to the next part of their day, the next date in their diary, the next item on their agenda. The world doesn't stand still for long. The funeral director - polished and shining like his car - waits in anonymous respect. He steps forward as he sees the two begin to leave the graveside, takes a step back as he sees them pause to talk.

'Mr. Johnston, Tom, I need to speak to you, another day, away from here. May I visit you on Saturday afternoon?'

He'd said yes to her. There was no reason to say no and no strength left to ask why.

~ ~ ~

Saturday Afternoon

There's going to be a baby. The girl is pregnant. Tom pottered about his garden repeating the words for no other reason than it helped to make the unreal, real. Was he speaking his thoughts out loud to the cabbages and the flowers, to the little dog digging a hole in the lawn without rebuke and, it crossed his mind, possibly also to nosey Barbara next door? He couldn't be certain that he wasn't. He also found that he couldn't be certain how he felt about the baby idea.

He wanted to know what Peter had thought when the girl had told him. Was he excited about unexpected fatherhood, or was he scared? Did he know the girl Debbie well enough to create family and security, and still be happy? When had he been planning to tell his old Dad about it? Too late for all those questions now of course.

Also too late to realise that the thoughts had indeed all been spoken out loud, because here was nosey Barbara coming out of her back gate, into the lane behind their houses and – uninvited - on in through his garden gate.

Then the voice boomed out,

'Thomas Johnston, are you going to be a granddad? Huh? Are you? Huh? Because if you are, then you just welcome that with open arms.'

And now here was the sight - crossed between scary and amusing - of nosey Barbara steaming down his daisy spattered lawn in her green wellies with arms held out from her sides, head high and gait purposeful. She reminded him of Joyce Grenfell reciting Stately as a Galleon. The galleon – and the military two-step - came to an abrupt halt.

'Thomas Johnston, you can be a lonely old man or you can be a granddad.' She stood in front of him, tall and statuesque, hands placed firmly on her hips, face covered with question marks - the splendid image marred only slightly by her having to squint against the sunlight.

'Well! What's it to be? Huh? You've been offered loneliness and you've been offered life.'

He hated it when Barbara turned all religious on him. It was embarrassing, made him think about things he didn't want to think about - God and church and all that kind of stuff. Barbara relaxed, which had the amusing effect of making her shrink. She shoved her calloused, gardener's hands into the pockets of her old, badly patched, and none too clean gardening jacket, looked down towards the ground in a gesture of uncharacteristic humility, pushed a stone along the path with her foot so that it rattled gently, took a deep breath. Then she looked into Tom's eyes, which became disconcertingly captive to her eyes, and said, so quietly that it was like a whisper in a dream, 'Choose life, Tom, choose life.'

There seemed no need of a reply, and after a moment Barbara turned briskly like a solider on the parade ground, stepped forward with her right foot, paused and then marched out of his garden, along the lane and back into her own garden. Without breaking step she marched up the path, raised a hand briefly in salute, and went into her house.

He knew that the bible quote was really *you have been offered life or death, choose life,* but he also knew that Barbara was afraid of death, or more probably, he pondered, afraid of how the world would possibly manage to keep itself in order without her in charge.

'Daft woman,' thought Tom, of course he would welcome Peter's baby, and its mother. Why would she even think he wouldn't?

Granddad - he tried the word out and discovered that it sounded good in his head.

~ ~ ~

October 2014

They stand side by side at the grave. The woman – Debbie - short and round, head covered in unruly greying curls dancing uncontrolled in the autumn breeze, the young man – her son Gregory - tall and straight, uncomfortable in the unfamiliar suit, arm across his mother's shoulders for comfort, for support, in grief, in thanksgiving, in hope.

'Earth to earth, ashes to ashes, dust to dust, in sure and certain hope of the resurrection to eternal life,' the clear ringing voice of the vicar rises above the traffic and the cheerful voices of nearby school children, released from their lessons for playtime. She is wrapped in a long black cloak against the wind and drizzle, which Gregory thinks causes her to look like a Victorian mourner. She's young and has a smiley face that Gregory finds unexpectedly alluring. He's not sure whether it's ok to think of vicars as alluring at a funeral.

'Did Tom believe in God, resurrection, eternal life,' Debbie muses to herself? 'Funny how you can know someone so well, and yet still not know important stuff about them.'

Behind them a familiar voice - designed to boom but clearly being held in restraint by a supreme effort of will - declares, *'The Lord gives and the Lord has taken away.'* A hand falls heavily on Gregory's shoulder, before being transferred with a thud to Debbie's. Even with her bowed frame and her walking stick Barbara remains stately. She pushes her head between the two of them, looks between their shoulders into the grave and onto the coffin, covered now with clods of earth and a few unseasonal roses. She continues in an uncharacteristic whisper which neither of them has ever heard her use before, *'Blessed be the name of the Lord,* Tom my old friend. *Blessed be the name of the Lord.'*

Then she's gone, swinging her stick bravely, marching across the grass. The mother and son are left alone at the side of the grave. Debbie takes the long, thin, smooth hand of her son between her own hands. Gregory feels the reassuring touch of his mother's short, dumpy fingers, a touch which has lost its familiarity over the years of his adulthood. She looks up at him, and his eyes are drawn down to her familiar face, where grief now abounds,

'Since the day you were born, Son - you were all the world to Tom.'

Gregory rests his chin on the top of his mother's head, encloses her in his strong young arms, feels her arms tight around his body,

'And he was all the world to me, Mum. He was all the world to me'

Silence

When words are wearied

ideas have released their hold

minds and hearts are set free

to hear truth, then

sit with me in the silence.

Speak not, we

are the other side of words.

Think not of what you would say, could say,

might say,

for in the end it is

only silence

that speaks truth.

Now we are Nurses

At ten o'clock in the morning on September 14th 1978 Nancy Williams found her way through the corridors of Cheltenham General Hospital and, along with nineteen other girls, gathered in The Board Room on the ground floor. Along the length of the polished wooden table in the middle of the room bundles of uniforms were waiting for them. The room was bright and airy with a high ceiling and large windows on two sides. In the small, tidy garden, which the room overlooked, late summer sunshine was dancing off the turning leaves.

The girls' new tutor, Mrs. Richardson - soon to be known by them all as Mrs. R – stood tall and straight, hands clasped behind her, apparently pondering the garden while she waited for her group to assemble. She had thick, greying hair swept into a beautifully created chignon and, they saw when she turned around, an open, friendly face.

Once her head count told her that everyone had arrived Mrs. Richardson introduced herself then went to one end of the long table and picked up the first bundle of crisp, white, starched aprons and blue and white stripped dresses. The bundle was topped with caps made of white card adorned with a single blue line, and a navy blue belt made of stretchy fabric with a small metal buckle. She held the bundle aloft and said,

'Nurse Clark?'

This was a shock to Nancy and, she later discovered, to most of the other girls. Nobody answered. Twenty pairs of eyes looked at the floor or the wall. No one looked at Mrs. Richardson, whose face changed from its busy, but impassive, expression to a jolly, twinkling smile.

'OK girls, from today you're all nurses,' she said. 'I'm really hoping that one of you is going to own up to being called Nurse Clarke.'

A short girl with chestnut hair neatly bobbed and fringed above dark brown eyes raised her hand and said in a quiet, anxious voice,

'I think that's me, Mrs. Richardson.'

'You think it's you,' said Mrs. Richardson. 'Well nobody else is claiming to have that name so I guess it must be you.' She smiled as she handed the bundle over to the newly minted Nurse Clarke.

Nineteen more uniform bundles were handed over as twenty girls each adjusted their head to the sound of their new title.

Nurse Edwards, tall, with thick straw-coloured hair hanging down her back in a plat, tied with a blue ribbon. Nurse Gates, calm and serious, receiving her bundle with a surprising degree of reverence, a little dip of her knee and an awed, 'thank you Miss.' Nurse Sysome, hopping from foot to foot as her bundle approached - which caused Mrs. Richardson to inform the group that should they need the facilities they could be found through the door in the corner, along the corridor, on the left; no need to ask permission, this isn't school. This caused a considerable amount of merriment around the room. Nancy's bundle came last.

'Nurse Williams,' said Mrs. Richardson, looking directly at her, 'that must be you then.' Nancy thanked Mrs. Richardson and took her bundle. She ran her fingers over the smooth cotton of the dress on the top of the pile, feeling the fabric-covered buttons and folded down collar; then she felt the starchy stiffness of the white aprons underneath. The uniform bundle felt like a gift, a gift which produced an awesome – and unexpected – feeling of pride in Nancy's whole being. She turned to the girl standing next to her and saw her own smile reflected in the other girl's beaming, freckle covered face.

They each took the top dress from their pile and shook it out. Some girls held their dress up against themselves. A few jostled for a look in the only mirror. A general kerfuffle of activity followed as each girl changed into her uniform. There was much merriment accompanied by more jostling at the mirror. Mrs. Richardson declared herself generally satisfied with the result – although Nurse Benyon's dresses would all need shortening somewhat, and Nurse Tomkins would need a slightly larger belt. She demonstrated how to adjust the belt, how to fold and clip on the cap, how to pin on the apron. She distributed hair grips for caps, safety pins for aprons, and name badges.

Nurse Jefferson – tall with a large angular face and a serious expression – deftly scooped her long hair up into a bun and, without the use of the mirror, secured it neatly. Nancy hadn't thought about how she would deal with her own long hair. She felt her face reddening with awkwardness. Holding her hair in both hands as she tried, without success, to imitate Nurse Jefferson, she called,

'Mrs. Richardson, I'm sort of stuck here.'

Mrs. Richardson was clearly well used to this sort of scenario. She produced a box of hair clips in every shape and size, and left Nancy to the care of the more expert Nurse Jefferson.

After this followed Mrs. Richardson's tour of the hospital. First, the locker room on the top floor - large and a bit gloomy with small, high-up windows - filled with tall, grey, metal lockers. Keys were distributed. Nancy found her locker close to the door and next to Abi Collins – small, sturdily built with a smiley face and a cheery laugh. Next, where to go if you were unwell while at work, 'sick bay girls; try not to use it.' Then which office to head for if your pay failed to arrive in your bank account at the end of the month, 'accounts office girls; be nice to them.' The Porters Lodge, 'be very nice to the porters girls; you'll need them often.' Then followed the chapel, casualty, out-patient clinics and the corridor to the ground floor wards, 'more wards on the next two floors, girls; same layout as this.'

And lastly the cafeteria, 'lunch time girls, I'll meet you back here in forty minutes.' Over lunch first names were exchanged and snippets of life stories shared. Abi's older sister was a nurse in the hospital, as was Barbara's mother - they both had stories to tell. Some of the girls lived at home with parents, while others had moved into the nurse's home. Two girls were married and living in flats nearby, which rather surprised Nancy who had assumed that they would all have just left school. Shirley was twenty and recently back from her honeymoon in Greece.

'Oh it was so beautiful girls; warm sunshine, beautiful beaches and best of all - no parents.'

Claire was the oldest of the group at twenty-two and already the mother of, 'my beautiful boy, Jacob. He's so gorgeous. But oh dear me the birth! I tell you never again, girls, never again.'

When Mrs. Richardson came to collect her group exactly forty minutes later, she was pleased to see that they were all happily chatting and laughing together, as she had anticipated they would be. Before they became aware of her approaching through the busy cafeteria she saw Nancy stand up, raise her tea cup in a toast, look around the group and declare,

'This, girls, is the first day of our nursing careers. May there be much fun, friendship and adventure to come our way in the years ahead.'

Nurses Haiku

Short rite of passage
dress cap belt locker, new friends
we're all nurses now.

Sunday Afternoon

Sunday afternoon on a hot August day; the hottest August Sarah could recall. At three o'clock she stepped out of the kitchen door, walked across the lawn to the shady place beneath the big tree, laid out the old cotton blanket on the grass, positioned the cushion – an ugly object with a faded Union Jack on, left behind when her son moved out – and arrayed her drink, snacks and book in a pleasing pattern at the edge of the blanket. Then she looked fleetingly at the red stone wall of the church – with its ugly and ill-fitting bell tower – looming large the other side of the garden fence. She gave head-room to a passing thought as it searched for a resting place, and was just a little surprised to discover that the words pleased her, gave her a sense of freedom.

'Sometimes I hate all of you.'

So powerful was the sense of freedom that came with the thought that she grasped the bottom edge of her tee-shirt with both hands and raised her arms to the sky, taking the tee-shirt smoothly over her head and then dropping it on the blanket. Where her tee-shirt had gone the rest of her clothes followed. As her body – somewhat surprised and not a little alarmed by this unaccustomed turn of events – felt warm sun in places more used to the comfort of cotton and the warmth of wool, that sense of freedom was tangible. Freedom from clothes, freedom from long held constraints – mother, modesty, morality – but most of all freedom from those people represented by that ancient, red wall with the ridiculous tower clinging to it like a grossly over-sized limpet.

She lay down.

A happy hour ensued – a little sip of wine, a few crisps, another sip of wine, all of the chocolate that was beginning to melt. She read a few pages of her novel, a book she had found on her mother's bookshelf which was proving to be pleasingly enjoyable. The wine – a rather larger glass than she was used to of a Sunday afternoon – was helping the sun to induce a sleepiness which she chose not to struggle against but to drift gently along with.

In the happy oblivion of dream-world there were apples with legs strolling across the lawn, a rabbit family lay on their backs sun-bathing and quoting nonsense verse to each other in French. The apples morphed into her children who squabbled good-naturedly while picnicking on bananas mashed into onion gravy.

And then, without notice or warning, there was a noise so invasive, so intrusive, so piercing, that even the sleeping Sarah knew that it had no place in peaceful dream-world. She lay rigid and still. And yes, there it was again, not part of the dream but horrible reality.

'Helloooo! Are you there Vicar? Helloooo!' Two heads peered over the garden fence.

'Is she there, Doris?' said the shorter head.

'Hold on a minute, Madge, while I just...' the taller head replied. Shuffling and scuffling, huffing and puffing followed.

'Hellooo Vicar helloooo. Are you there vicar?'

The taller head, elevated with the aid of a convenient bench, peered out from the midst of purple and white hollyhocks, looking herself, thought Sarah, now awake and on alert, like a giant hollyhock with that gaudy hat and those ridiculous sun-glasses.

Slowly, ever so slowly, Sarah reached for the edges of the old cotton blanket, pulled it gently over herself, and rolled from her back to her right side, to her front, to her left side, until she was underneath the weeping of the willow tree. Her face was resting on crisp crumbs. Melted chocolate was lodged in her hair. The wine glass – she was surprised to observe – was clutched in her left hand. The book, which could not alone provide evidence, was unaccounted for. In this cocoon Sarah felt herself invisible – if rather hot and lacking in air.

'Is she there, Doris?' Sarah heard Madge's insistent – but now muffled – voice.

'Help me down, Madge, help me down.' Doris' urgent plea was accompanied by renewed shuffling and scuffling, huffing and puffing.

'Oh my good gracious me! Whatever next! Come along, Madge. Come along.'

'What is it Doris? What did you see? Was she there?'

Sarah unwound herself from the blanket, stretched languorously, propped her head back on the patriotic cushion, retrieved the book and, with a certain sense of contented satisfaction at the outcome of the neatly avoided encounter, began to read.

There was a Young Vicar from Bude

There was a Young Vicar from Bude,
who liked to lie out in the nude.
She was seen by old Dot,
who was quite the fusspot,
declaring 'that's ever so rude'.

Winter Weddings

It seemed to Anya that, although winter was not the most usual season for weddings, this was turning into a winter of weddings.

Today she was her best friend's bridesmaid, and just now she was standing in the porch of St Chad's Church. She was in charge of two small page boys and one even smaller flower girl, as they all waited for the arrival of the bride. The December day was dry and bright but there was a sharp wind blowing across the flat, open churchyard. She was wearing a long, floaty, pale pink dress made of a fine gossamer fabric, with a low neck and sleeves so short they may as well not be there. Her arms were covered with the thinnest silk scarf – or was it a pashmina? Whatever it was called she considered it not very satisfactory as a winter garment.

At the dress fitting back in September she'd tried to raise the small matter of the British winter, and the strong likelihood of less than clement weather, with Cheryl, today's bride.

'Won't we be cold in thin, sleeveless dresses with tiny shawl thingies in the middle of winter, Cheryl? The heating in that old church isn't going to be great.'

Cheryl, whose own dress was equally lightweight, equally low-cut, and almost sleeveless, and whose own shimmering silver and white scarf/pashmina was designed for photos not warmth, had grabbed Anya's arm, a huge excited smile on her face, and laughingly declared,

'Of course we'll be cold, Anya, freezing probably. But won't we look gorgeous?'

One of the ushers came out to see how events were progressing at what he called, 'the girls end of things.' Anya recognized him as a lad called Peter who had been at school with her brother. Peter was a friend of the groom at last weekend's wedding – when Anya had also been a bridesmaid – and, apparently, he was a friend of this week's groom as well.

'Oh. Hi Anya,' said Peter, 'good to see you again. I'm an usher this time around. Not really sure what I'm supposed to do but hey ho nobody seems to have noticed.'

Peter laughed. He looked at Anya, put his head to one side, folded his arms, nodded slowly, like an ancient Sage, pursed his lips, then said to her,

'Well now, look at you, Anya. Always the bridesmaid.....'

Then he went back inside the church, chuckling to himself. Anya felt very cross with him. For the rest of the day she avoided him. She stood well away from him during the photos and, when he asked her to dance at the reception, she declined in what she hoped was a brusque and off-hand manner. She felt vindicated to see a hurt look cross his face and she remembered that they had danced together at Meredith and Samson's wedding, just last weekend.

'Good,' she thought, 'I don't need him being rude to me and laughing at me.'

~ ~ ~

Meredith – last week's bride – was Anya's cousin. When they were ten, and it became clear that neither of them was likely to acquire a sister, they had promised each other that they would be like sisters to one another, and that when they were grown-up they would be each other's bridesmaid. In the following twenty years Anya had rather gone off the idea of being anyone's bridesmaid, but Meredith held true to her childhood promise and so, when Meredith asked Anya to be with her on her wedding day as chief bridesmaid, Anya found that she couldn't say no.

At that wedding there had been a warm, and very cosy, registry office in the nearby town where Meredith now lived. Anya had worn a long-sleeved, layered, royal-blue bridesmaid dress, which she considered to be sensibly warm, with a beautiful, pearly-blue, alpaca-wool cloak, which Anya just loved. The ceremony had been followed by a short – but adorable – reception in the hotel down the road from the registry office. There had been fizz and tapas, more fizz and cake, and a lively jazz band to dance to. Peter, she recalled, was a good dancer. They had had fun.

~ ~ ~

Two weeks after Cheryl's wedding – just a few days before Christmas – Anya had a phone call from her friend Judith.

'Oh Anya, hi how are you? I've got a really big favour to ask you. You know how our wedding's on Christmas Eve?

Judith paused briefly but not long enough for Anya to say more than, 'yes, looking forward to it'.

'Well, I'm in a pickle, Anya darling. Naomi – you know Naomi who's my bridesmaid? – well she's only gone and got appendicitis. She's in hospital. Probably getting operated on as we speak, poor girl. Please please please, lovely Anya, will you take her place for me? I'd love you to be there with me.'

Judith paused again. Then she sniffled. Then she said in a quiet voice, 'you're one of my best friends.' Another pause. Then something like a quiet wail accompanied the words, 'and you're the only one the dress will fit.'

Anya was interested to realize that she wasn't in the least offended by this. She loved Judith and had known her a long time. This wedding was long planned. It had been cancelled twice, the first time because of the pandemic, which threw everything into disarray, and the second time because Judith found herself pregnant. She was so in love with her –admittedly very beautiful and very expensive – wedding dress that she couldn't think of wearing a different, roomier, dress, and so the wedding was postponed until three months after the birth of her large and raucous baby boy.

'Of course I'll be your bridesmaid,' said Anya. 'I'll come over this evening if you like and try the dress on. We'll have a little glass of wine. I'll bring a few nibbles. I'll see you at eight o'clock.'

A jolly three days followed. The dress proved to be a tad tight and a couple of inches too long. The re-hemming was completed the day before the wedding, but the tightness would just have to be endured. The very attractive hair decoration – chosen to adorn Naomi's thick curls – refused to stay on Anya's short, fine hair whatever they tried, so after much hilarity, Judith decided that it could be abandoned and tossed it unceremoniously behind the sofa. The shoes – rather higher heels than

Anya was accustomed to wearing – were, mercifully, her size.

On the evening before the wedding Anya and Judith were enjoying a nice glass of chilled Chardonnay with Toby – tomorrow's groom – and Steve – Toby's Best Man – when the doorbell rang. Toby jumped up.

'That'll be Peter,' he said.

Anya knew, before Toby came back into the room with the new arrival, that this was going to be the same Peter. And it was.

'Peter, this is Steve who's my Best Man, and this is Anya who's Judith's new bridesmaid. Peter is chief usher tomorrow,' said Toby, while waving his arms vaguely in everyone's direction by way of introduction.

'Hi Mate, good to meet you,' said Peter to Steve. Steve lifted his glass of wine in response. Then Peter turned to Anya, did a mock bow and said,

'We meet again, Anya the bridesmaid.'

'Good grief,' thought Anya, 'he sounds like someone from a Victorian novel.' In the interests of wedding eve harmony she gave the briefest of smiles and did a little wave with her free hand. The next day, at the wedding, she avoided him and he seemed to be avoiding her – which Anya was amused to realize she found a little irksome. There was no invitation to dance.

~ ~ ~

The fourth wedding that winter was her brother's. Anya was hugely relieved not to have been called on for bridesmaid duties this time around. Bernice – her soon to be sister-in-law – had an abundance of sisters and best friends, so although there were six bridesmaids adorned in shell pink dresses and loose fitting ruby jackets, Anya was not one of them. And this time she felt that she was prepared. She knew that Peter – yes, the same Peter – was to be her brother's usher.

The wedding party gathered in the entrance of the Town Hall, which was a huge, ugly building on the high street of their home town. The ceremony room itself was lofty, spacious and attractively decorated. When it was time for the ceremony to commence, and they were called in by the registrar, Peter was holding open the door to the room, welcoming people, showing them where to sit, being all jokey and smiley. As she went past him Anya paused just long enough to look directly at him and say,

'Hello Peter, always the usher……'

The wedding was beautiful. Anya decided that all weddings were beautiful. She was so happy to see her brother laughing and smiling and holding Bernice close. In fact she was so happy that at the reception when Peter asked her if she would dance with him, she said that she would. When he asked her again later in the evening she heard herself saying yes again. When the evening was drawing to a close and the last dance was announced, she crossed the room to where Peter stood, beer in hand, and said,

'Why don't you put that drink down and come and dance with me?'

~ ~ ~

And so Anya and Peter danced. They danced their way through many a Saturday evening at the small nightclub in town, with its horribly loud music. They danced their way through alternate Wednesday evenings at the Jazz night upstairs in the Red Lion. They danced in her kitchen. They dance in his living room. They had great fun dancing at the silent disco in the huge cathedral in the nearby city. In the summer they went on holiday to Gran Canaria and, after days spent sight-seeing, poking around the flea markets, swimming and sun-bathing, they spent the evenings dancing in the hotel bar, or by the poolside. When they arrived home it felt odd to leave each other and go to their separate homes to prepare for work on Monday morning.

'Such a wonderful holiday,' they said.

'We had so much fun,' they said.

'See you on Wednesday then,' they said.

'I'll miss you,' they said.

'I love you,' they said.

And so, as February turned into March, they danced their way right up to the parish church where, sensibly clad in warm winter-wedding clothes, they made their vows to each other in the presence of their families and their friends.

Cheryl, once again looking gorgeous in a thin floaty dress, cradled her baby girl, and beamed at Anya. Meredith, enormous but radiant, with twins due any day, fell asleep on a sofa at the reception missing the speeches and toasts completely. Judith, now the happy mother of a second, equally raucous, baby boy, had a relaxed air of experienced motherhood about her. As they cut the cake, listened to the speeches, hugged their guests and danced with each other, Anya cradled her own secret – which she had decided she would share with Peter later that evening.

Wedding Haiku

These two joined by vows
to honour love cherish, till
death draws them apart

Make me proud

They're choosing the body tonight. History will be told the lie that no one else was here. History will be wrong. I am here - generally making myself useful - and Frank is here. But in truth I'll be invisible to them. Oh they'll see me. But then as well, they won't see me.

I like to think that's because I was a good soldier, discreet, deferent, humble even, 'yes sir no sir'. They think it's because the likes of me don't really matter, just one more man to be kicked around as the glorious British army thinks fit. Really it's because we're all weary - bone-chillingly weary - emotions mashed to pieces. We've seen humanity taken to the brink of madness and dangled there by the devil incarnate. Wrecked; all of humanity is wrecked; the whole world has lost its dignity. A few tiny threads of civilization remain, and out of those we are all now striving to rebuild the earth we have destroyed.

November 1920 and the world has ceased its insane spiralling out of control, has brought itself to a place of regret and sorrow, and so I am here in this place with rows of bodies that used to be men, covered with flags. Too late for them any expression of regret or sorrow; too late to ask forgiveness; too late to tear down Kitchener's boldly pointing finger from every wall and fence and hoarding; too late to rip it from every newspaper and magazine. Too late to scream no no no this is madness. Surely any of them would exchange this honour to feel once again the soft embrace of a mother, a sister, a sweetheart.

It wasn't meant to be like this. We started out with such hope, with such a sense of adventure, 'over by Christmas,' they said, and we believed them. We were just boys trying to be men, now some are dead – some days it feels as if most of them are dead, the lads from school, the lads from the works - and those who aren't dead are men wishing they were still boys sleeping soundly at night, untroubled by nightmares. Whichever poor sod they choose here tonight the dead can't wish for anything. 'Age shall not weary them nor the years condemn.' I bet they wish it bloody-well would.

‘Hey Bert Bert, look smart there, Bert, the brass hats are here.’ Frank’s voice, urgent and excited, breaks into my thoughts.

We stand together near the wall in the shadows and watch silently, hardly daring to breathe lest we be noticed and told we had no place there. But we had a place there all right; any one of those bodies could be my Charlie or Frank’s brother Jack. Let either of them two fellas try saying we had no place there and I’d be giving them a few choice words of my own to take home with them.

Frank senses my anger and I feel his hand clamped to my shoulder like he’s saying, ‘not now pal.’ That’s his left hand; his right one’s been lost on some bloody battle-field. They’ll take him for the handyman – we’re all careful to be polite to the resident cripple these days. ‘Lest we forget,’ that’s what this whole palaver’s about, ‘lest we forget.’ Not much bloody chance of Frank forgetting. Sixty years from now he’ll still be waking up every morning minus an arm.

So here they are, Brigadier General Wyatt and Lieutenant Colonel Gell - all arms intact - walking through the chapel in their death-solemnity. Wyatt takes a step forward, bows his head like he's praying; maybe he is, we mostly all did a lot of that during those hell-years. He chooses a body, then the two of them - Wyatt and Gell - lift that chosen body into the waiting coffin.

'The nails please,' the General says. Gell hands them to him and there's tapping of metal on metal until the lid's well and truly hammered down. They stand back and salute, and somehow I end up holding the hammer and nails. My head's shouting out, 'don't treat me like your bloody batman, I'm a solider too,' but the words can't find their way out. I've seen terrified men flogged for less in the trenches, and terror dies hard.

And so the deed is done. The Unknown Warrior is chosen. Maybe it's Charlie, maybe it's Jack. Most likely it's some other poor bugger. Before we leave we look at the brass plate screwed on top of the coffin. It says, 'A British warrior who fell in the Great War.'

'He didn't fall,' I say to Frank, 'he was bloody-well pushed.'

'Come on Pal,' he says, 'time to leave.'

~ ~ ~

Bert crouched along in the cold trench. This one was hopelessly shallow, duck boards resting on inches of mud, a haven for the rats. He reached the dug-out and hunkered down inside cursing the Sarajevo bullet ricocheting around Europe like it didn't know how to stop. Cursing Fritz dug into his own trenches, so close he could hear him snoring when he wasn't pounding them with his rage and his bullets. Bert balanced his cup on a stone – the tea now tepid from the rain-water – and reached into his pocket for his letters. Nothing from Mother and Dad today, one from his old school-chum, Cecil, home on leave, and one from Freda. He supposed Freda was his sweetheart. He supposed they had what Mother called 'an understanding.'

He leaned his head against the wooden post. His eyes opened and closed in an ancient dance with sleep. Thoughts of Fritz mingled with thoughts of home. Freda flitted in and out of his dreamland, smiling her sweet smile, offering him a kiss on the cheek, holding out her white feather.

'This is for you Bert. I hope it'll make you think hard and do your duty. Make your mother proud Bert, make us all proud.'

He tried to fight his way back to the real world, but Freda and her white feather held him fast in dreamland.

'This is for you Bert. Make your mother proud Bert, make us all proud.'

Later, when he was woken by the artillery fire getting closer, he thought,

'Well it's not Freda Jackson that's covered in mud and lice, weary to the bone, hobbling with trench-foot, head banging from the endless firing, stuck in clothes you've not taken off for a week, feet swollen and bleeding into wet boots. Does this really make you proud, Freda Jackson?'

'Take them boots off and you'll never get them on again,' Frank had said, weeks ago now. Some of the fellas laughed at him, but he'd been right, now those same fellas were going through the bodies packed into the walls of the trenches, looking for bigger boots that their owner no longer needed.

When Bert woke again from the same familiar dream of endless marching, it was with a dread that this was all that life would ever hold for him now. The sun was yet to find its way over the horizon, he was bathed in sweat, engulfed in fear, seeing in his mind the fellas from the Forest Pals, not knowing – in those waking moments – who had made it through this far, and who hadn't. And always, always, just before dream-world turned into real-world, there was Freda Jackson in a spotless pink dress and jacket, smelling of Pears soap and violets, saintly smile on her face, head held on one side, holding out her white feather to him.

'This is for you Bert, this is for you'.

In those moments of waking he could smell the blood and the mud and the bodies, he could hear men beginning the day, and the voices of fear hidden by bravery – or more likely by the fear of not being brave. And every day at that moment of waking Bert took that white feather from the, lace-gloved hand of Freda Jackson.

'Make me proud Bert. Make us all proud.'

~ ~ ~

I'm sure our soon to be famous unknown warrior made some girl proud; saddened the heart of some mother; sent some father into a spiral of despair and pain which will never end. But today he takes a journey back over the channel that he never asked to cross in the first place. I've heard there'll be a nineteen gun salute from Dover Castle, impressive huh? And there are sure to be crowds to welcome him home, as he makes his way through London to his overdue funeral –which is more than most of the men got - and his illustrious place amongst the great and the good. And there he will be, for years to come, every girl's brother, every mother's son, every young lass's sweetheart.

~ ~ ~

The day of the big offensive the whistle blew at dawn, heavy, obedient boots pounded up the ladders, men scrambled over ditches thick with mud, stumbled over burst sand-bags, fell onto clumps of barbed wire.

When they went over the top most of the fellas were hoping for a Blighty if they were honest, something to get them out of that hell-hole. Frank was with me when we left the trench, and our Charlie was there on my other side. Charlie shouted,

'Right lads, all together now,' and grinned like it was some kind of cowboys and Indians game that we'd played in the garden, back when we were boys, but really it was just bluster. He was as scared as the rest of us. Those were the last words I heard him say. Then we were gone, striking out into what had once been No-Man's land, surging into the gunfire and the shelling, into the shouting of men and the screeching of horses. Men cut down as they went over. No time for screaming. Only the reek of blood and churned up earth, the stench of fear and explosives, no way back, only forwards into the carnage. Falling over bundles of khaki that had once been men, desperate to keep upright, smelling death all around, knowing it was coming our way. Knowing we were sending it the way of the Hun.

The next thing I remember seeing was our Charlie plastered onto the barbed wire, his head hanging sickeningly off his shoulders. I knew he was dead, and my heart and my head cried out for my brother. I tried to reach him - tried to bring him back - but a shell slammed into the ground right beside me. I felt my guts rip to pieces. The pain and the impact sent me reeling and bouncing along the mud.

I crawled. I crawled foot by agonizing foot along the ground for what felt like all the hours of a day. I was heavy with mud, trying to clutch a hand over my side where the shrapnel went in. I could hear screaming. I was trying to block it out. Maybe some of it was mine. I could feel the warm stickiness of blood seeping through my uniform, seeping through my fingers, mixing with the mud.

'Keep going keep going Bert keep going' it was like a litany in my head. 'Keep going Bert you're alive keep going.'

Suddenly, like some kind of a mirage, like some kind of miracle, there was Frank standing over me.

'Bert Bert is that you? Aw mate you don't look good. Can you stand up…? Here lads, over here, help me with this fella. Get him up on my back can you? He's in a bad way. I'll carry him.'

I felt trembling hands and weary, hurting bodies lift me onto Frank's back, and as they did I saw that his one arm hung useless by his side, the sleeve torn away, what remained of the hand hanging ragged and raw, like something in a butcher's shop-window.

'You're gonna have to hang on tight there, Bert lad, this one arm's done for; ole Fritz took a swipe at it.'

The clearing station was packed, men everywhere, groaning, crying out, lying down in despair, wandering around in confusion. An exhausted nurse was sorting through us all as we arrived, this one for the surgeon, this one for bandaging, this one for the train, this one no point bothering. Me and Frank both made it to the surgeon, where Frank lost what was left of his arm and I said goodbye to most of the bits of shrapnel stuck in my belly.

~ ~ ~

By the time they reach us at the hospital the men are all bone weary. The journey is long and tortuous. Some days the trains will stand for hours in a siding waiting for the next batch of gun-fodder to pass along the track on its way to the front; the wounded are not the priority. There's tea and water and food, although some of them just throw it all back up again, and there's endless hours of pain with nothing to do but try and sleep. It took this batch seven days to get here, seven days of a lesser hell, in and out of the trains, on and off the boat, still in the clothes they were injured in, tormented by lice, the reek of blood and vomit everywhere.

When they arrive here…. well… it must feel like heaven on earth, mustn't it?

'Righty-ho, young man, let's get these clothes off you and get you cleaned up and into bed. What's your name?'

'Bert, Nurse, my name's Bert.'

'Well, Bert, my name's Gladys, Sister Gladys …. How old are you Bert?'

'Twenty-two, Nurse, Sister, Sister Gladys. I'm twenty-two.'

'Do you have a sweetheart back home Bert?' I always ask the men that when they arrive, I feel it takes their minds off their injuries for a while, brings a nice picture into their heads. Sometimes the thought reminds them that they've got some letters from home tucked away in their kit bag, and when I'm done with them - and they're all neatly settled in bed in clean pyjamas and clean bandages - they get out the letters and read them. Helps them settle in you understand, helps them to rest – to start being a patient and stop being a solider for a while. Which - you must agree - can only be a good thing?

'Freda … her name's Freda. Pretty she is, Sister. Wears pink dresses and those little pill-box hats the girls like. Curly brown hair. Smells of violets and Pears soap.'

'Well then, you must let Freda know that you're here. Maybe she'll be able to come and visit you.' Visitors are good for the men, when the visitors are here they stop all that endless talk about the conflict. Although, of course, visitors do also bring their own distresses, with news of brothers, friends and neighbours lost to this pointless war.

I worked away with my usual efficiency. I'll be thirty-five next week, older than most of my nurses. I was a nurse before the war and I'll be a nurse when it's finally run its course, and so I like to set a good example. 'We can't be delicate,' I tell my nurses, 'and we must never find the men's injuries repulsive. They need us to be kind, but they need us to be sturdy too.'

I myself have always been sturdy, emotionally and physically. I suppose I'm considered tall for a woman - nearly six-foot - and I've never allowed myself to be squashed into dreadful fashionable corsets. 'I can't work if I can't move,' I told my mother many years ago. I had no intention of wasting my life on sewing and afternoon-tea and husband-hunting, facts of which I apprised her very early on. My rather bemused father stood by my decisions – although I believe he thought they would pass - and now I know that I am both intelligent and educated. I earn my own living and I'm beholden to no-one.

I also have a passion – courtesy of my grandfather – for the game of chess. It's a game that I've taught to several of my patients – partly so that I can have opponents, and partly to ease them through those hours when the terrors of the battlefield visit to torment them, like the demons of old. It's a game that I taught to Bert.

~ ~ ~

'There comes a time in some games,' I declared, continuing to look at the board, 'when no one can really win. There are plenty more moves left to be made and the opponents can play for hours, but in the end no one can really win.'

I looked up. Bert's face was serious, more serious than its usual seriousness. Our eyes met each other's in a new and unexpected way. Somehow I felt his brain, his mind, his heart – I'm not sure which – take a seismic leap. He said, 'Like this God-forsaken war, Gladys?'

I held his gaze; felt my lips pressed together in a parody of a smile. My hand covered his as it lay on the table.

'Like this war, Bert, like this war. But as to whether it's God who has forsaken man or man who has forsaken God … I no longer know.'

We stayed that way for a while, our eyes seeking meaning, or truth, or some other undefined need, our hands, both large and strong, gripping each other; deep in our shared thoughts.

'I'm going back as a man who just wants the whole thing over and done with, Gladys. I'm not the boy wooed by the propaganda and the romance of it all this time – caught in the trap of the white feather.'

'Come back safe, Bert .... Come back safe.'

'May I write to you, Gladys?'

I stood up, no longer looking at him, and began to move the chess pieces back to their starting places. Men were coming into the room now, chatting and smoking, looking around to see if tea had arrived yet, opening the big doors onto the garden, cheered by the brightness of the sunny afternoon; someone put a record on the gramophone and Caruso's voice drifted around the room.

'I wish you would, Bert, I really do wish you would.'

~ ~ ~

And so he had. Just short letters, just once a week at first. He told me about the horror of life in the trenches, with the mud and the rats and the cold, the reek of acetone that heralded cordite and the elusiveness of gas, the stillness amidst noise and the daily deafening fear. He told me about the days behind the lines with the simple joy of tents to sleep in, hot baths and half-decent food. He told me about how he must watch friends die and unknown men go mad, of how he grieved for Charlie, of how he missed Frank's company.

In late March 1917 he told me he had leave coming up and of how he would go to see his family; of how he would go to see Freda.

~ ~ ~

France

May 8th/17

Dear Gladys

Mother and Dad were well and we were able to say goodbye to Charlie together in our own quiet way. We gave away his clothes and some other of his things and cleaned and decorated his room. Mother has put a photo of him in his uniform in a wooden frame on the sideboard, with the cross she kept from Palm Sunday. Every family has its own loss and we have, I believe, found our peace with ours.

Freda and I seemed to have little to say to one another. Our experience of war is so different, and I believe I have changed so much.

I pray this whole damned business is over soon.

Kindest regards

Bert

~~~

France

November 30th/17

My Dear Gladys

We have a chess set, Gladys. One of the men has whittled it from old bits of wood and I am once again able to lose a few idle hours engrossed in tactics and strategy. I'm remembering what you used to say about the
~~~

importance of a plan in the middle game, and the difficult balance of the endgame. Once again I'm sacrificing pawns to save kings, and all those other ploys you taught me. Some days, Gladys, I think it's like you said, that a game of chess is just like this game of war that we're playing – only in this game maybe we're all pawns.

I'm sorry that so much of my letters is falling foul of the censor's pen, but I think that you can guess my thoughts well enough, and also, dear Gladys, it does help me to write them down even if they are never to be read.

My very best regards

Bert

~~~

France

October 10th/18

My Dear Gladys

I heard news today that Freda is to marry our old school-chum Cecil, who has been invalided out (he always did have a weak chest). I find myself completely at peace over
~~~

this. Freda is a fine girl, but we have moved so far apart over these years. She holds to her belief that the war is needed and that the lives lost have been what she calls, 'a needful sacrifice.' I now see only pointless destruction and slaughter – much as I believe you do Gladys, much as you do.

Anyway, it seems that the war is drawing to a close – the chess players are finally admitting the end, Gladys –and there is now every possibility that I shall make it back safely.

You wrote that the hospital there is closing and that you will return to the infirmary. Be sure to send me your address, dear Gladys, I should like to visit you once I am home, if you will allow me to. Your letters have meant so much to me in my many dark hours. Is it alright to say that I treasure them?

Kindest best wishes

Bert

~~~
~~~

France

December 5th/18

Dearest Gladys

Do you remember back when I was at the hospital, you told me that chess is just a game of skill that anyone can learn? Well, myself and the rest of the men still out here are beginning to feel that we've mastered the skill of war – we are at least still alive while many good men are not.

Thank you for sending your new address. I expect to be home in about four weeks. It feels good to know I will be starting the New-Year back on English soil, and even better to know that I will soon be out of uniform. I shall come to visit you just as soon as I have spent a few days with Mother and Dad. I so look forward to giving them both a hug, and dare I hope for a hug from you as well, dearest Gladys?

Fondest love

Bert

~~~
~~~

The battle-fields had long since ceased their clamour; their dead were given up for burial, or disappeared forever beneath the lime. There was a silence in the world hewn out of regret and sorrow; the time of mourning was passing, the time of lament was just begun.

It was late afternoon on a cold day in early December 1920. The seasons had travelled around to meet themselves twice since the guns were laid down. Inside the abbey the atmosphere was damp, the lighting dim. Most of the day's visitors had left taking their whispers and their dreams with them –'maybe he's my son, he could be my brother, perhaps he's the one I was to marry' – taking with them also that endless and unending question, why? Why did it cost so much, why so many good lives gone forever? Why would it never be worth the price it had demanded? Why why why?

'Beneath this stone rests the body of a British warrior.' Gladys was reading the inscription on the gravestone.

'Look at this,' her voice was indignant, 'in the presence of His Majesty King George V. So that would be the same King George who said the whole idea was abhorrent when the good Reverend Railton proposed it?'

'Distasteful,' Bert replied, 'the king said the idea was distasteful.'

'That's as close as makes no difference, Bert.'

'Thus are commemorated the many multitudes,' Bert read aloud. He turned to look at Gladys, as if waiting for her to share her wisdom with him – he felt he would always, hereafter, wait for Gladys to share her wisdom with him, - 'who gave the most that man can give…'

'History will judge this generation harshly, Bert, we can be sure of that. We've done a bad thing, and even once we knew it to be bad, we were somehow not able to stop it… of course, not everyone acknowledged it to be bad, I suppose.'

Bert read on, 'they buried him among kings because he had done good towards God.'

'Gladys, is that not a blatant disregard for the sixth commandment? How can all that killing be seen as something good towards God? How can it, Gladys, how can it?' Gladys felt the anger rising inside Bert's body, working its way to his head, waiting to explode into wrenching tears and angry words. She turned to face him. She was as tall as him, in fact just a little bit taller. She put her arms around him, held his head in her palm until their foreheads rested together, each dusting the other's face with cold winter breath, her voice was low and caressing as - in a now familiar pattern - she soothed away the anger, soothed away the pain. She felt his body relax as his arms held her close.

'Don't ever leave me, Gladys. The world scares me now. I can't find my way without you. Don't ever leave me?'

Gladys held his face between her palms, wiped the tears away from his cheeks with her thumbs; gently kissed him.

'Bert, listen to me. It is just one week, since I promised to love and honour you, for better or worse, in sickness and in health, and all those things. I'll never let you go, Bert. I'll never let you go.'

Dreams filled with the dead

The war that failed to end all wars

when humanity tasted blood in a new way

an ocean of blood, rivers of mud,

washing away arms and legs,

sight and sanity.

Minds once sound twisted now

with memories which can't be washed clean

by time

or love.

Dreams filled with the dead

for fifty years

or sixty

or seventy

Acknowledgements

Thanks to all those who have helped this book to become a reality, for your encouragement, for your belief in my words and for your support.

A new book will be on its way soon.

LC

Lily Craske publishing

Printed in Great Britain
by Amazon

25635218R00061